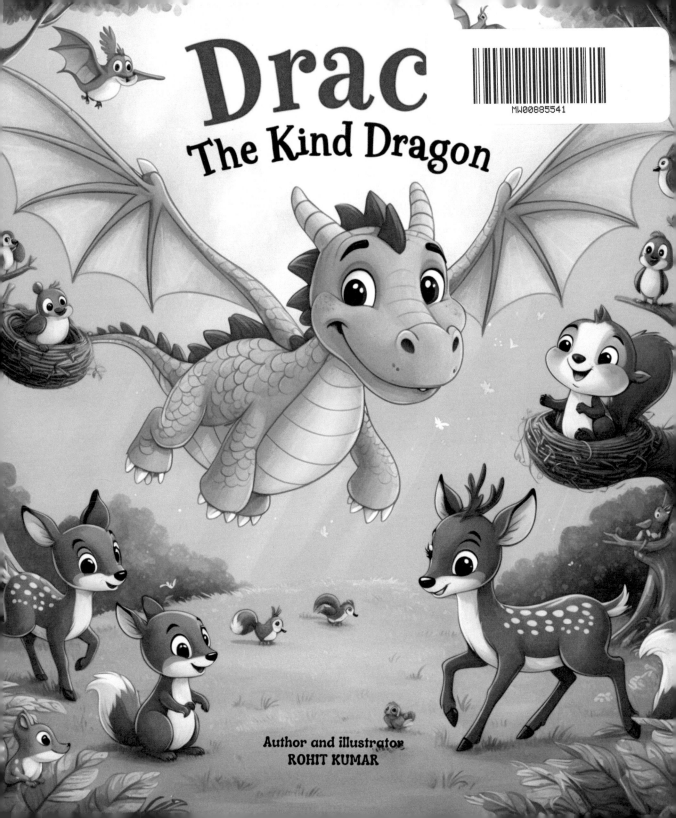

Drac
The Kind Dragon

Author and illustrator
ROHIT KUMAR

Copyright © 2024 by Rohit Kumar

All rights reserved. No part of this book may be reproduced, distributed, or transmitted in any form or by any means, including photocopying, recording, or other electronic or mechanical methods, without the prior written permission of the publisher, except in the case of brief quotations embodied in critical reviews and certain other noncommercial uses permitted by copyright law. For permission requests, write to the publisher at the address below:

Copyright © 2024 by Rohit Kumar Printed in UNITED STATES OF AMERICA

First Edition ISBN: 9798341396821
KINDLE DIRECT PUBLISHING author-rohit kumar
rohitkumarverma5656@gmail.com

In a land of trees so high,
Lived Draco, a dragon who loved to fly.

With wings so wide and scales
so bright,
He soared above, a gentle sight.

He wasn't fierce, he wasn't mean,
Draco was kind, calm, and clean.

He'd help the birds build their nests,
And guide lost creatures back to rest.

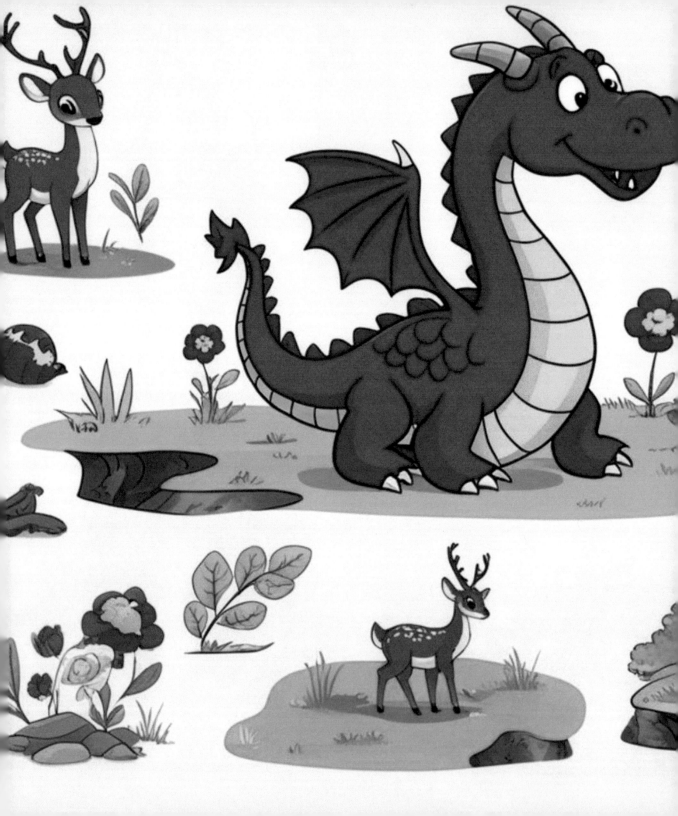

One day he heard a tiny sound,

A baby deer was on the ground.

It slipped and tripped near the hill,
Draco flew fast, strong and still.

He scooped it up with gentle care,
And flew it safely through the air.

The baby deer gave a
happy cheer
"Thank you, Draco,
you're so dear!"

The forest animals soon all knew,
Draco's heart was pure and true.
Whenever trouble came to stay,
Draco would chase it all away.

But one day a storm began to blow,
The sky was dark, the wind did grow.

The animals feared, ran to hide,
But Draco stayed right by their side.

With a mighty flap, he calmed the skies,
And dried their tears with his big eyes.

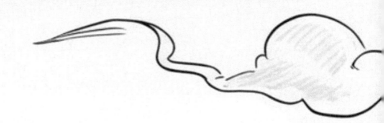

"Don't worry, friends, I'll keep you warm,
Together, we'll brave this mighty storm!"

When the clouds cleared and sun
came out,
The forest cheered, they all did shout:

"Thank you, Draco, you're so brave,
For keeping us safe from the wave!"

And so the dragon's tale was told,
Of Draco's heart, pure as gold.

Not all dragons are fierce or fight,
Some spread kindness, day and
night.

Made in United States
Troutdale, OR
10/29/2024

24229548R00024